LOST IN SPACE™

Adapted by Judy Katschke

From a screenplay by Akiva Goldsman

SCHOLASTIC INC.

New York • Toronto • London • Auckland • Sydney

ISBN 0-590-18936-0

Photos by Jack English and Milly Donaghy

12 11 10 9 8 7 6 5 4 3 2 1   8 9/9 0 1 2 3/0

Printed in the U.S.A.
First Scholastic printing, April 1998

Designed by Nancy Sabato

It's hard enough moving to a new town— can you imagine moving to a new planet?

The Robinsons, a family of scientists, are about to find out what it's like. It is the year 2050 and they will soon travel aboard their spaceship, the *Jupiter 2*, to a planet called Alpha Prime. They will become the planet's first settlers.

It took the Robinsons three years to train for the mission. Professor John Robinson would be the commander. His wife, Maureen Robinson, was a biologist, and in charge of life sciences. Judy, their older daughter, was the mission doctor. Fourteen-year-old Penny would handle video mechanics, and ten-year-old Will would take care of robotics. With such experts onboard, what could possibly go wrong?

One day before the launch, Professor Robinson described his mission to the media: "My family and I will sleep away the ten-year journey to Alpha Prime frozen in our special cryotubes," he explained. "Once there, we will begin to build a hypergate, a kind of doorway in space."

Reporters scribbled in their pads as Professor Robinson went on. "By then, technicians here on Earth will have completed the companion hypergate. Once both gates are finished, spaceships will be able to pass between Earth and Alpha Prime instantly."

The reporters knew how important the mission was. Earth's natural resources were depleted, and in twenty years the planet would no longer be capable of supporting human life. Humans would have to move to Alpha Prime if they wanted to survive. The Robinsons and their Robot were pioneering the way to a new world.

"How do your children feel about the mission?" a reporter asked.

Professor Robinson smiled. "They couldn't be more excited!"

"This mission stinks!" Penny told her mom. She hated the idea of leaving Earth and everything she loved: orchids, popcorn, a boy named Billy.

The one thing Penny refused to leave behind was the wrist video recorder where she recorded all her thoughts and secrets. "My video journals will make me world famous one day," she told Will.

For Will, life on Earth was pretty cool. He had just won first prize in his school science fair for a model of a time machine.

And with his trusty hacker deck, a miniature computer, he could do anything—zap out the school lights, even make his principal look like a hairy gorilla, holographically, that is.

The one thing Will couldn't do was get his dad to spend more time with him.

Not all the Robinson kids gave the mission thumbs down. Judy was looking forward to keeping the crew healthy once they took off. But the crew of the *Jupiter 2* was not complete.

The pilot had been shot down the night before by members of the Global Sedition, an enemy group that hoped to reach Alpha Prime before the *Jupiter 2*. A new pilot was needed right away.

"I want a pilot who's more than just spit and polish," Professor Robinson told a U.S. Army general.

The general nodded. "I've got your man!"

That man was Major Don West, a brave fighter pilot who had risked his life in space to save a friend.

"It's a baby-sitting job, sir," Major West complained. "Any monkey in a flight suit can pilot the ship!"

But then Major West checked out the fancy controls of the *Jupiter 2*.

Not too shabby . . . if you have to baby-sit!

As the Robinsons spent their last night on Earth, trouble brewed aboard the *Jupiter 2*. His name was Dr. Zachary Smith.

The Robinsons knew Smith. He was their base doctor. What they didn't know was that Smith was a spy for the Global Sedition. He was onboard to reprogram the family's Robot.

"My orders are to protect the Robinson family," the Robot said.

Dr. Smith typed madly on the keyboard. "Let's see if I can change your mind."

"Robinson family. Destroy. All systems. Destroy," the Robot suddenly said.

Smith smiled. "Now that's more like it!"

But on his way to the exit, an electrical charge knocked him out. Dr. Smith didn't know it, but he was trapped aboard the *Jupiter 2*.

Launch day finally arrived. After suiting up, the Robinsons took their places inside the special freezing tubes.

Judy checked the systems while Will and Penny had their final fight on Earth. "Maybe we can cut back on Penny's oxygen so she's not so creepy when she wakes up," Will suggested.

"Does Will have to wake up at *all*?" Penny asked her mom.

Judy contacted Mission Control. All systems GO!

Major West watched the tubes close around the Robinsons. A white frost covered them as they drifted off into their ten-year sleep.

"The Robinsons are tucked in. We're ready to fly!" Major West told Mission Control.

The dome parted. The base of the saucer exploded. The spaceship shot through the clouds into deep, dark space.

"I never liked these tubes," Major West said as he prepared to chill. "Bad dreams!"

But the crew's worst nightmare was only a few feet away.

Dr. Smith awoke at last. He climbed out of the chute he'd been trapped in. Where was he? Then he realized. He was onboard the *Jupiter 2*, on his way to Alpha Prime! Suddenly he heard a loud CRASH!

A huge, hulking shape burst from the wall. It was the Robot Dr. Smith had reprogrammed earlier. The Robot was following the doctor's orders.

"All operating systems, destroy. *Jupiter 2*, destroy." Dr. Smith tried to get close enough to shut off the Robot, but he could not. So he hid in a corner as the Robot fired at the controls.

The freezing tubes opened and the Robinsons and Major West woke up. "Robinson family. Destroy."

Professor Robinson shot at the Robot. The unharmed Robot fired back, knocking him against the wall.

Will had to do something—fast! The Robot fired at Will as he ran through the spaceship and disappeared onto an elevator going down.

"Will, wait!" Maureen shouted.

The Robot slowly turned to Maureen and Penny. Electricity shot out from his claws.

"Robot. Return to your docking bay," came an order.

It was Will, the tiny hacker deck in his hands.

"Command accepted," the Robot said.

Will grinned proudly. He didn't win the science fair for nothing!

"Show-off!" Penny said.

Major West heard a groan and spotted Dr. Smith huddled in a corner. "What are you doing here?" he asked. "You caused this trouble, didn't you?"

And the trouble wasn't over yet. The *Jupiter 2* had been knocked off course during the struggle with the Robot and was now heading straight for the sun!

"If we can't go around the sun," Major West told Professor Robinson, "we have to go through it." The crew held on as Major West engaged the hyperdrive and daringly piloted the ship through the fiery ball. After a wild ride, the *Jupiter 2* came to rest in an alien universe.

"We're lost, aren't we?" Penny asked.

A huge hole in space shimmered before them.

"Where does it lead?" Maureen asked.

There was only one way to find out. Major West headed the ship toward the hole.

"Major! Wait!" Professor Robinson ordered.

"I'll wait later," Major West said stubbornly. The ship passed through the mysterious hole. On the other side was a spaceship with an American logo! But it didn't look like any ship they had ever seen before.

"This place smells of ghosts," Smith said as he followed Judy, Major West, Professor Robinson, and the Robot onto the spaceship. Maureen, Penny, and Will stayed behind on the *Jupiter 2*.

Inside they found a strange room filled with flowering plants and vines. It looked like a jungle. All of a sudden, a tiny creature popped out from under the vines. Major West grabbed it. It looked like a funny little monkey, but it was covered with scales instead of fur.

"Blawp. Blawp," it cooed.

Unfortunately, not all the creatures onboard were so cute and friendly.

Hanging out from holes inside the ceiling and waiting to attack were . . .

SPIDERS!

Giant space spiders half the size of humans with sharp, steely bodies and dripping fangs. The monsters jumped down on spindly legs. Major West fired at them, but it was no use. The ship was crawling with the giant alien insects.

"Evacuate. Now!" Professor Robinson shouted. The crew tried to race back to their ship, but before they made it, a door slammed shut in front of them. They were trapped!

The Robot came from behind and blasted a hole in the door. Judy, the alien creature, Major West, Dr. Smith, and Professor Robinson all ran through it to safety.

Using his bulky body, the Robot blocked the opening, protecting the crew from the charging beasts. The spiders clung to the Robot's back and started to eat his body.

Will had been giving the Robot commands by remote control.

"Leave him behind," Professor Robinson told Will.

"Good-bye, Robot," Will said sadly. "I'm sorry."

One spider made it past the tattered Robot.

"Seal the door—now!" Professor Robinson ordered as the spider swept its razor-sharp talon through the opening.

Suddenly, the little alien jumped across Dr. Smith's back. "This tiny horror scratched me!" Smith howled. He didn't know the scratch was from the hideous space spider, not from the creature.

The crew was safe for now, but Major West didn't want to take any chances. "I hate spiders!" he shouted.

Against Professor Robinson's orders, Major West blew up the alien spaceship, spiders and all.

The exploding ship released a mighty blast wave into space. The wave hit the *Jupiter 2* and sent it spinning into the atmosphere of an icy planet below.

"Hang on," Major West warned. "It's gonna be a bumpy landing."

The *Jupiter 2* touched down. It skidded on a giant crater sea. Then it crashed to a stop against a crater wall.

Now they were *really* lost in space. And the *Jupiter 2* was damaged.

"Half the radioactive core is burned out," Major West said. "Without it, we'll never have enough power to lift off."

Later, Will sat alone at the main computer console. He felt bad about the Robot and vowed to rebuild him. Luckily, he had saved the Robot's mind.

"Robot tried to destroy the Robinson family," the Robot said. "Why did Will Robinson save Robot?"

Will shrugged. "I guess sometimes friendship means listening to your heart, not your head."

Will wanted to rebuild the Robot right away. "Mom always said I should try to make new friends," he said.

And speaking of new friends. . .

"I promise I'll always look after you," Penny said, stroking the tiny creature she'd brought from the other spaceship.

"Blawp. . . Blawp."

"That's what we'll call you," Penny said. "Blawp!"

Things looked gloomy for the *Jupiter 2*.

Loud rumbling noises filled the atmosphere. The alien planet the ship was on seemed to be breaking up.

Professor Robinson had a theory. "The rumbling might be caused by opening and closing doorways to the future," he told the crew.

"Awesome!" Will exclaimed. "That's exactly what my time machine is supposed to do."

Professor Robinson shook his head. "This is not the time for flights of fancy, son."

"You never listen to me," Will cried, storming out. "Not ever!"

Professor Robinson wanted to follow Will but time was running out. How long would the planet last?

Maureen detected radioactive material that could save the ship. Professor Robinson and Major West had to find it fast.

Will watched his father leave. What if he didn't come back?

Seconds later, the Robot delivered a message from Dr. Smith:

"DANGER, WILL ROBINSON, DANGER."

Dr. Smith convinced Will that Professor Robinson and Major West were in trouble.

Will agreed to follow them off the *Jupiter 2 and* into the future with Dr. Smith.

Professor Robinson and Major West passed through many doorways in time. Each one led them further and further into the future.

Finally, they found the source of the radiation signal: an old, broken-down spaceship. It was *their* ship—the *Jupiter 2*—way in the future!

"What kind of nightmare is this?" Major West wondered out loud. Suddenly, a powerful blast hit him in the back.

Professor Robinson ducked and fired his laser. Then *he* was hit. He looked to see where the shot came from and saw a Robot!

The Robot was not alone. A man with a shaggy beard and mustache came forward.

"Who are you?" Professor Robinson demanded.

"Don't you recognize me, Dad?" the man asked. "I'm your son . . . Will."

And the Robot was the one Will had rebuilt.

Will's dream of building a time machine had come true, too.

"I'm going back in time. To stop our family from going on this mission," the older Will explained. "I'll save us all."

But there was someone else who wanted to go—Dr. Smith.

"Don't move, Professor Robinson," Dr. Smith warned. He kept a rough, tight grip on the younger Will's arm as they entered the ship. "Or this strange family reunion will be short."

"Never fear. Smith is here," came a new voice.

Smith spun around to see a repulsive monster. The spider scratch he had gotten on the other ship had turned him into a creature that was half spider and half man. This was the doctor's future self.

Future Smith grabbed the doctor and hurled him through a hole in the floor. "I never liked me anyway!" he said.

Then he ordered the Robot to take three prisoners: Professor Robinson, Major West, and the younger Will.

Future Smith had plans of his own. He would be the one to travel to Earth in the time machine. Once there, he would take over the entire planet. But first he needed to get rid of the older Will!

"Time to die, son," Future Smith said. Then he knocked out older Will and pushed him out of the way.

Meanwhile, the Robot kept a close watch on his captives.

"Robot, don't you remember what I taught you about friendship?" the younger Will asked.

"Friendship means acting with your heart, not your head," the Robot said.

"I need you to help us now, Robot," Will said hopefully. "Because we're friends."

"Friendship does not compute," the Robot told Will.

"Please, Robot!" Will cried. "If you don't let us go, we're all going to die!"

The Robot lifted his claws. He ripped off his controls. He had remembered Will's lesson after all.

"I will save Will Robinson. I will save my friend."

The prisoners were free to return to the past, and to the *Jupiter 2*.

"I'll try to get the radioactive core material and meet you there," Professor Robinson told Major West and the younger Will.

But when Professor Robinson reached the console, he found he had company. Future Smith was waiting for him. Professor Robinson slammed into the giant insect/man, sending him backward over a railing and into the flames surrounding the time machine.

Professor Robinson watched as the flames swallowed Future Smith. But just as he was about to go after the core material, he saw another figure: The older Will was hanging over the fiery basin where Future Smith had just disappeared.

Professor Robinson could save the core material before it sank into the console . . . or he could save his son.

In a flash, Professor Robinson reached for older Will's hand.

Back in time, the crew of the *Jupiter 2* worked to free the ship from the crater wall.

"We're not getting any altitude!" Major West said.

Penny pointed to the roof of the hull. "Look!" she cried.

The roof swirled to reveal Professor Robinson and the older Will.

The older Will had used his time machine to get his father back to the spaceship.

"Don't forget me!" he called down. He pushed his

father through the time doorway and into the *Jupiter 2*. Then he slowly disappeared.

Back on the ship, the younger Will approached his dad. "I'm glad you came back," he said.

Professor Robinson gave his son a big hug. Will smiled. A hug from his dad was better than all the science fair medals in the world!

"The planet is breaking up around us," West interrupted.

Without the radioactive core to lift the ship into orbit, there was only one way to go—DOWN!

Gravity yanked the *Jupiter 2* through the planet as it began to break up.

Major West piloted the ship past flying slabs of molten rock. "Rock and roll!" he cried.

The *Jupiter 2* burst through the mouth of a volcano into the black of space.

Will and Penny glanced back. The strange world behind them exploded into a million pieces.

Space had never looked so good to the Robinsons and Major West.

With the help of a star chart Will had made, the *Jupiter 2* headed once again for the planet Alpha Prime.

But then a blast wave from the exploding planet hit them from behind. Major West had to use the hyperdrive to get away fast. "Here we go again," Penny said, and the *Jupiter 2* vanished into hyperspace.